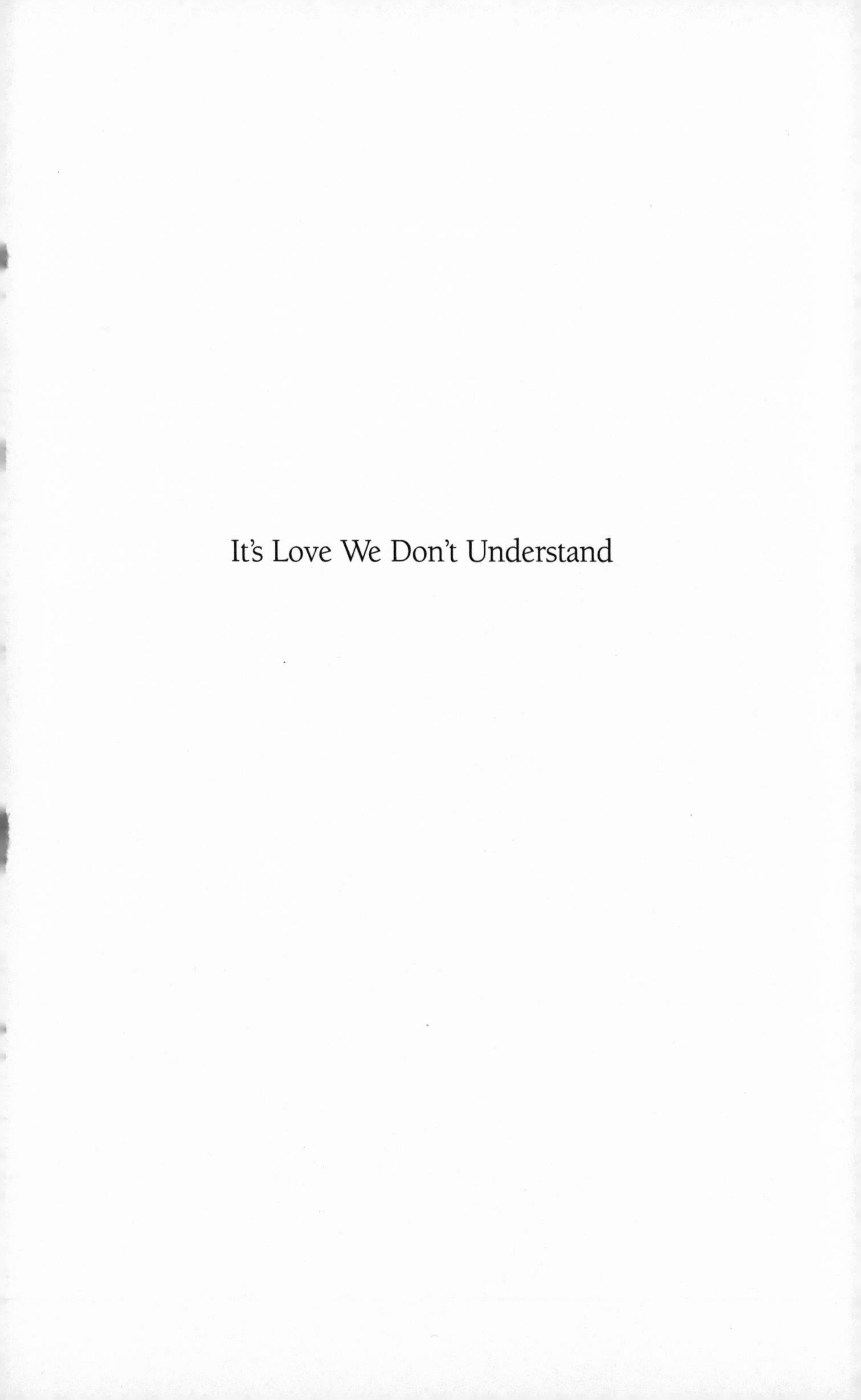

It's Love We Don't Understand

It's

We Don't Understand

BART MOEYAERT

translated from the Dutch by

Wanda Boeke

FRONT STREET
Asheville, North Carolina

Also by Bart Moeyaert

Bare Hands
Hornet's Nest

First published in the Netherlands under the title
Het is de liefde die we niet begrijpen
by E.M. Querido's Uitgeverij B.V.

Designed by Helen Robinson
Printed in the United States of America

First edition

The translation of this book is funded by the Flemish Foundation
for Literature—Vlaams Fonds voor de Letteren

Library of Congress Cataloging-in-Publication Data

Moeyaert, Bart
[Het is de liefde die we niet begrijpen. English]
It's love we don't understand / by Bart Moeyaert;
translated from the Dutch by Wanda Boeke.
p. cm.
Summary: In three episodic scenes of their family life,
a fifteen-year-old girl describes the troubled interrelationships,
alternating between love and hate, between herself and her
siblings and their self-absorbed, neglectful, and often absent mother.
ISBN 1-886910-71-5 (alk. paper)
[1. Family problems-Fiction. 2. Abandoned children-Fiction.
3. Brothers and sisters-Fiction.] I. Boeke, Wanda. II. Title
PZ7.M7227 It 2001
[Fic]-dc21 2001059776

The End of Bordzek, Told by Myself Who Was There

In the curve, Bordzek slumps against me like a brick. His head drops forward and I can't move anymore. I can't punch him because my hand is stuck under his rear end and my shoulder is caught between the seat and his upper arm.

On my right sits my mother, who is herself looking for a spot for her arms and saying to me, "Move up a little, would you, girl?" and between my legs Bordzek's dog scrambles to his feet for the hundredth time. Everything is panting in here. I get my elbow to move, but it doesn't have much strength and the space I gain isn't much.

Bordzek's bare skin, there where his shirt is not in his pants, sticks to my arm. I would like to bop his dog in the snoot with my knee, to make him lie down, lie down dead if possible, but I don't dare. Maybe Bordzek sleeps with his eyes open.

The road runs through fields. The wheat is yellow and the sky above it moves. The windows in the front are open, but hardly any breeze comes in through them.

My brother has hung his left arm out the window. The other hangs loosely over the steering wheel. His forehead shines. Even his eyelids are sweating. In the piece of his face that I see in the rearview mirror, there is no expression. He is not with it today. At most he's part of the steering wheel. He doesn't give us any warning. He doesn't say, "We're stopping here." He simply puts his foot on the brake.

Bordzek's dog falls over, Bordzek himself slumps against the door with a grunt, and my mother braces herself by spreading her legs. The upper part of my body flies forward and finally I get some air.

The car comes to a standstill in a hollow of wheat. The engine shuts off and after that there is no more sound, not of birds and not of the highway we must be very near. Through the open window, the heat falls in like hot mush.

My brother opens the door, hesitates, hauls himself out of the car using one hand, and groans as he straightens his back. The driver's seat groans too.

For a while my mother and I sit and stare at Axel from the back. There are circles of sweat under his armpits, between his shoulder blades, between the cheeks of his butt. He takes a couple of steps forward, then stands in front of the car with his hands on his hips.

The passenger seat squeaks. Edie takes a look over the top edge. She has been quiet the whole way. She is still glowing a bit, she's so proud she's allowed to sit up front. The child is six and will die dumb, I sometimes think. We'll be lucky to hear her last breath. She looks at my mother and at me, as if she were comparing my mother to me, and slides back down into her seat.

"We'll be on our way soon," I say to her. I look sideways at my mother, who puffs, popping her lips as if they were swollen.

Bordzek's dog can no longer find any peace now that

we're stopped. He yelps and squeezes himself between our legs. I lean across my mother and push the door open. The dog can't get out of the car fast enough. In a single bound, he leaps onto the grassy shoulder and disappears into the field.

My mother looks from me to a point somewhere in the distance, scrunches her handkerchief in her fist, lifts her own heavy leg, and sets it down on the ground outside.

"If he says nothing's wrong," she says.

In her mind, her sentence is complete.

I pinch my lips together. Oh, Mother, I think. If somebody says nothing's wrong, it doesn't really mean that nothing's the matter. Some mothers prefer to be deaf and blind.

She draws up her other leg and gets out. As if in slow motion she walks around the car while she plucks at her pants and through their stretch pulls her large panties from between her cheeks. She goes over and stands beside Axel. Shoulder to shoulder they stand, and from their backs I can tell they're not saying anything to each other. I wish they would, they've been avoiding each other for so long, but they don't move and steadily the insects outside start buzzing louder.

I can't stand being in the back seat anymore. I bounce to my feet as if springing out of a little box and stand beside the car. I have to squeeze my eyes half-shut because of the sun.

Bordzek's dog cuts a trail through the field. Wherever he runs, the wheat tosses back and forth. If he is looking for the car at this point, he is going in the wrong direction.

I bend my knees a little and look inside the car. Bordzek is sleeping. His head is glued crookedly to the window, and his mouth has dropped open. His black jacket, which he laid on his knees when we left, lies crumpled at his feet.

"My," says my mother all of a sudden. "My goodness, boy."

I raise my head so that I can see over the rounded roof of the car, and my breath catches in my throat. My brother is leaning against my mother. I think he's crying.

He doesn't make a sound, though. My mother either. She has put her hand on the middle of his back.

Edie opens the door on her side. Her head comes out first. She looks pale. She slides out of the car as only she can. She is her own shadow.

I pull her toward me by her arm and push the door between us shut.

"We'll be on the road again soon," I say, and I take her hot hand. "But first we're going for a walk. A nice long walk."

My mother looks over her shoulder and quickly nods in my direction. Yes, that's good. Yes, you take care of that child.

I pick Edie up, and in between us it immediately starts to swelter. With her arm around my broiling neck and under my hot hair, her small body against me, in some places I become almost liquid. I hold firm up to the top of the low rise, there where the road goes down again. There I have Edie slide to the ground against her wishes, and I wipe the sweat from my eyebrows. I shield my eyes with my hand and look to my left into the sun and see trembling wheat as far as I can see. I look to my right, where farther on there is a scrap of a bush, and after that I look around once at the car. On purpose I stand with my back to it, but Edie doesn't do that. She doesn't want to miss any part of what is happening between Axel and my mother. They are still leaning against each other.

"Come on. Come on, this way," I say to Edie, and I pull her along by her dress to a narrow path that leads down, in the direction of the bush. Farther on there is green and shade and probably coolness as well.

Edie takes large and small steps, flattens dried-up clumps, and after a few feet seeks my hand.

I look at her. "Soon we'll drive just a few more minutes, maybe," I say. "And then we'll be at Bonnie's."

She looks up and smiles as if she were happy for me.

I can't tell from her face if she herself is happy too.

Behind me Axel suddenly shouts a couple of incomprehensible words. The sound of his voice startles me. The blood in my body rushes to my head. The words were very close by, but my brother is farther away than I thought. I turn around and see Axel opening the door on Bordzek's side.

"This gentleman here!" he shouts at my mother.

What at first I'm not expecting happens anyway. Bordzek falls out like a sack of potatoes. The side of his face smacks the ground, and his big body follows. He still makes a grab at the air with one hand, but there is nothing for him to hold on to. I feel pain in my own bones, slap my hand over my mouth, hold back the sound in my throat.

"Ow," says Edie.

I believe I pinched her by accident. She is rubbing her upper arm and looks to see if a black-and-blue spot is growing there.

My mother wants to go over to Bordzek. My brother bars her way. He holds her back using two hands. She'll have to fight if she wants to reach Bordzek, but she'll go to great lengths for him. She defends herself, with her mouth at first. I can hear her cursing all the way from here.

"Leave him alone," she hisses at Axel. "You're to leave him alone!"

Bordzek has taken an ugly fall. He is holding his face and doesn't get up right away. He is probably lying there yammering all kinds of things in his broken English or his unbroken Polish.

My mother lends weight to her curses with her hands. She twists and turns and makes claws of her fingers, but Axel keeps her away from him. Her arms are too short. She can't manage to scratch him. She keeps it up until it's pathetic, but her nails don't come near his face.

"I'll do what I want with my life," she yells a few more times. Her rage gives her added muscle. She balls her hands into fists. She punches around wildly. I think there is spit flying out of her mouth.

Axel's hand hesitates for a moment but suddenly strikes her in the face. She is knocked back, falls against the car, keeps herself upright with her elbows. The body of the car must be hot. Her skin must be sizzling. She curses, scrambles to her feet, and dashes forward, throwing herself blindly at my brother as if she were setting her shoulder to a door.

"Ow," says Edie.

I look down. This time I didn't pinch Edie. No, she sees just as I do how Axel hits the ground. We feel pain for him. I don't think about it for more than a second. I jerk Edie around by her shoulder and push her ahead of me.

"You know what? We'll go on foot," I say.

"Yes," says Edie.

"That's right," I say.

I give Edie a little push, but she doesn't put up a fuss. She never puts up a fuss. She steps onto the grassy shoulder beside the wheat field—she doesn't hesitate for an instant. I think she has seen enough. I almost grab her little collar so she'll lead me, because I can't resist: I do look back. I strain my neck, almost lose my balance, want to keep seeing the car as long as possible.

Bordzek is lying on the ground. Axel makes motions to get up. The last thing I can still see is my mother's head, red with rage, and the way she raises her arm to lend weight to the hand she wants to hit Axel with, but after that the wheat is too tall.

I look ahead of me. Edie and I are walking between

two straw walls. The grass is stuck to the edge of the wheat field, and the wheat is glued to the sky above it.

I wonder if Bordzek has meanwhile gotten up. Maybe he angrily jumped on Axel, or maybe he crawled over to my mother on his knees, or maybe the three of them are shaking hands—they're sorry, they're sorry that they let themselves go like that, and can't they talk things out now, although I don't think they'll do that, none of us are very good at talking things out.

Somewhere a lark sings and a couple of crickets chirp, but the sound is no louder than paper tearing. The sudden sound of our car engine is much louder. On the other side of the wheat field, Bordzek's dog starts barking excitedly.

"Axel?!" I hear my mother exclaim.

I hold Edie back. I myself stand still too, as if I were nothing but an ear. I hold my breath. Something in the air is as quiet as we are. Something is waiting for more. Something that is big as a balloon, something that is waiting to burst. It can't take any more air.

Behind the wheat field our car starts moving. At first

it sings, it always does that. I expect it to gain speed, but instead it slows down. It stops. I feel my jaw drop. I turn my head in the direction of the noise. The air in my throat stops.

The engine suddenly does the opposite of what it did just now. It doesn't sing nicely, it shrieks.

"Axel?" screams my mother.

I hear our car tear into reverse, tires squealing. It picks up speed in no time. The noise amplifies. In my mind I see what is happening on the other side. I see the car drive backward. I see Bordzek lying in the road. I hear my breath. I hear myself make a tiny sound, and it's as if that one tiny sound were too much. The air around us suddenly explodes with a cry from my mother and the squealing of brakes. The cry comes from down deep, as if it had been stored there for a long time, and in my mind I hear a thud that isn't a thud but seems like a thud because there is much too much silence after my mother's cry and the high-pitched sound of the brakes.

The whole place cringes. The lark has dropped out of the sky.

I notice I have my hands over my mouth. The inside of my mouth is dry. My voice is gone. I see that Edie is looking at me, I see that she is white around her nose, I see the way the corners of her mouth turn down, the way her lips are working, and I can't even say, "It's all right."

I pick Edie up and lay her against me, with her head on my shoulder. It was sweltering between us before, but now I like her being close to me.

I have to go back. See where my brother is. See what my mother is doing. See if Bordzek is lying under the car. I almost trip over my own feet, but I keep my balance and walk on rubbery legs to the scrap of a bush. On purpose I do not look too quickly at the spot where I suspect the car is. I get my eyes ready. First, they can see the sky, then the wheat, then the road.

Yes. Now.

There goes my mother. She is at the highest point of the road, where Edie and I just were. Her feet are already disappearing. She is clipping along for her. Her legs are already getting shorter. Her brains are probably melting, but her back is made of stone.

"Mother!"

She doesn't react. My brother can shout all he wants. She won't be coming back today. She clips along toward the other side of the world.

"Come back!"

Axel is standing between the car and the other side of the world. He holds his hands away from his body, as if they were grimy and he would otherwise get his clothes dirty. He looks at what is left of my mother, her moving upper half, which is getting shorter. He hesitates about whether to call her again, looks back at the car, then looks straight ahead once more.

I looked at the car along with him. I know what I will see again in just a minute. I push Edie's head to me so her face is lying against my hair, then look at the car.

Its doors are open. The front seat is empty. The back seat is not. Bordzek is just slumping onto it, legs sticking out. He is holding his hat in his hand. He lays his head to rest in it. The sky above him is blue, the wheat is bright yellow, and his blood is very red. From a distance, he seems to be bleeding everywhere, or maybe I'm only wishing that. His head has to be bleeding, his hat, his white shirt. He dabs his face with his handkerchief. It doesn't help. The handkerchief is also bleeding.

I follow Axel with my eyes. He has set off at a run after my mother, who is already waving him off because he went too far. With my eyes I'm at his heels up the low rise. If I could, I'd push him ahead. Then he'd be with my mother faster, and they would be able to settle everything once and for all. I just hope he comes back. I just hope he comes back with my mother. Of course he'll come back. He says it so often, my brother, that he cares about me and Edie so much. And we care about him very much, no matter what sounds we might hear him make at night.

Edie starts squirming. She wants to see what I see, but I press her against me by the neck, turn just my mouth toward her ear, and whisper that she has to be good.

"We don't know about anything, Edie," I say. "We don't know about anything. Seven times," and I give her little pats on her bottom with my free fingers. Seven pats on her bottom, seven times we don't know about anything. Everything seven times, because that brings good luck. That's how we always play.

"Momma and Mr. Bordzek and Axel are having a little argument," I tell her gently. "A terrible little argument, but it'll be over soon. It's better not to look. Can you try and sleep?"

Edie breathes. That's all. The child is in a box, I sometimes think. We have to make do with the thought that she exists. For the rest, she remains as closed as a package with a bow on it.

She pushes her little fists into my neck and moans deep down in her throat.

"Yes," I say in my gentlest voice, as if I were answering a question she posed. "Yes, we'll be on our way in a second, we'll be on our way to Bonnie's in a second. Sis will be happy to see you."

I feel Edie's lips curl on my cheek. She is smiling. I have to smile too.

"She'll be very happy," I say and I hope that Edie will keep her smile, if only for a couple of minutes. As long as she doesn't look for a little while, or falls asleep, that has to be possible in this heat, as long as she doesn't have to see Bordżek's bleeding face and my mother's rage or Axel's. A few more miles to Bonnie's and then everything will be fine again.

I sigh and step out of the shade of the bush. I cross my fingers, hope that everything will turn out, and hold Edie tighter. At each step I wish for Axel and my mother to pop up again there where the road is at its highest.

I don't see them anywhere. I run my gaze into the sunlight and down, then up again to the next highest point, but they are not to be spotted anywhere. There is no way they would have walked back to the highway without me and Edie. They might leave Bordzek behind—yes, he was the last to come into our lives, so he should be the first to disappear—but they can't leave us stranded.

I look in the other direction, at where we have to go. Our yellow car is standing in the fiercest heat. Just close the doors, Mr. Bordzek, I think. Suffocate. Take care of things yourself. Bleed to death.

There is the sound of barking from the field beside me. I see exactly where Bordzek's dog is running. He is going around in circles, just circles. He is too stupid to head for the road in a straight line.

I press a kiss into Edie's thin red hair and take a few hesitant steps in the direction of the car. I'll have to go. That's where I can sit, where Edie can lie down, because I believe she is getting heavy with sleep. She is floating on my sweat, that sweet kid. I am almost passing out from the heat on my neck, but I'll bear it for her. I am happy she wants to sleep in my arms and gives me the chance to care for her. That way I don't have to think of myself just now.

The sweat runs off my forehead. Now and then a drop inches through my eyebrows and slides down my cheek in such a way that it feels like a tear. The thought of tears is not a good thought. My throat constricts at the slightest thing. I have to swallow a couple of times. I have to walk faster. I try to think of other things, of how heavy Edie is getting, of how my knees are buckling. I think of the gray spots I see at the edges of my eyes.

I manage to sit down in the passenger seat without waking Edie. She lies across me like a blanket that is much too warm. She drools a little on my neck, I feel her small teeth press into my flesh, the big grown-up front teeth she just got, and the baby teeth, but I let her lie the way she is lying. I will think of her. That way half of Bordzek's scent will escape me and I won't hear what he is mumbling either.

His smell has filled the car, the scent of the gel he uses to glue his hair, the scent of his blood, his sweat too. With his big obtrusive body draped over the back seat, he lies panting, his legs outside and the upper part of his body sprawled in here.

I turn the rearview mirror so I can see him. I sit and study him for a very long time without his knowing it. In my opinion he's acting as if he were suffering. He has laid his head back, on the top edge of the seat, and now and then he opens his mouth to gasp for air, like an animal that eats meat, I think, because that's what he looks like a little bit, like something that is digesting meat. He has his eyes shut. He's not asleep, he's lying too uncomfortably for that. The wound on his cheek isn't as big as I thought. The blood has oozed just to his sideburns and only slowly thickens. He contorts his mouth, murmurs in Polish, and groans with his hand on his chest, as if his heart hurt. I can only hope that it's true. That it's broken. My mother is not with him. No, my mother is not with him. Axel is not with him either. No, not Axel either. Nobody is with him.

"Is it clear?" I say. My voice is fragile and I have to cough, so it seems as if I were afraid of him, but I'm not. I cough again. "Is it clear that we want you gone? Edie still doesn't think about things, the way I do, she has patience with everybody. But I do think about things, and I don't have that much patience. I've tried to act as if I liked you, but you're too much. The house creaks since you came." My voice trembles, but not from fear. It trembles because I am using words that I already thought but have never spoken aloud.

Bordzek blinks his eyes, slowly, as if the heat had made his muscles longer, and looks past the mirror.

"You shouldn't pretend you don't hear anything. You

do hear me, and you know that I hear you at night too. But don't worry, I won't say anything."

He closes his eyes.

Yes, he has heard me. Yes, he understood me. His eyes are shut. That's a good start. It would be nice if he were thinking with his eyes shut about what he is doing to our lives. Or to Axel's life. Now, if he would just bleed empty with his eyes shut and disappear from our lives all by himself.

Edie shifts in my lap. She thinks I am my mother. She rubs her face on my chest as if I had my mother's breasts. I look down, run my fingers through her hair.

When I look up into the mirror, Axel and my mother are walking behind Bordzek's head. A thick air moves around them, their bodies tremble in the heat, but they are walking back there. I look around and sigh with relief. They are closer than I thought. Axel is already almost at the wheel, and my mother is just about to get in beside Bordzek.

As soon as she is sitting, she sizes up Bordzek and his bloody head and shirt, and nods at him. When Axel has gotten in, she nods at him as well and, as if it were the end of a discussion, says, "I won't interfere with your life either. Deal?"

Axel looks at me.

I pull the corners of my mouth up, but I'm not smiling.

Axel's eyes say that he is still furious with our mother. They say that she gets on his nerves, but his eyes always say that. He grabs my knee and gently squeezes it. That's supposed to make me happy.

"Hey," he says to me.

"Hey," echoes my mother. "I said: deal?"

"No, Mother," says Axel.

My mother turns to face outside, toward the open door.

"Vlad!" she calls out to the wheat field. "Here!"

We sit without moving until Bordzek's dog comes panting up and jumps onto my mother's lap like a kind of grasshopper.

She sweeps him off.

"My life and your life are intertwined, Mother," says

Axel. “Things are the way they are.” He turns the key in the ignition, indicating that he doesn’t expect a reply. The car sings and roars. For the rest, people’s words are superfluous whether their lives are interwoven or not. The doors slam shut as if they never had to be opened again, and we all lurch back because of the way Axel accelerates.

I stroke Edie’s head.

Stop, I think the whole time. Stop. I almost say it out loud, but I am distracted by the slope of the road, by the curve we are taking, by Edie’s weight, and the thought of the red roof of my sister’s house.

Soon there will be cake. Soon Bonnie will pour out ice-cold near beer, which quenches the thirst better than real beer, and we’ll all be sitting around the table, panting, under the secondhand fan that throbs like a helicopter. Outside it will be hotter than inside, but then inside the air will be thick enough to cut with scissors.

With a little bit of luck, my mother will turn on the TV, and Bordzek will go lie down somewhere where my mother will go take care of him so that my sis and Axel and I can still have a little fun together. And with Edie, of course, but Edie always has fun quietly by herself, so she'll go climb a tree somewhere and build a hut.

I hope that Bonnie says blunt things. "Who hit him over the head with a board?" She's so crude that it's refreshing. "What did he scrape that face of his on?"

"On the road coming here, Bonnie," I'll be able to say, calmer than she is, so that I can feel older than I am, so after a while I'll be able to say really sensible things that will be worth something to me later on too. "They've been stewing over it for months, but don't ask me why today of all days they declared war."

"They're worse than children," Bonnie will say. "They should be stood in the corner and rapped on the knuckles."

"Yes, well put."

I'm nodding off as I look for the roof of Bonnie's house in the distance. It is still nowhere in sight. I think Bonnie lives closer than she does, every time, and every time it surprises me how far we still have to drive.

I am startled by Bordzek's dog, standing with his

front paws between the front seats. For no reason he mops his tongue over my upper arm. Drool drips from his mouth, and he's looking around as if he were the boss of us all.

"Enough," says Axel suddenly.

All of a sudden Edie is awake too. I think I gave her a nudge by accident. We both slide forward on the passenger seat because Axel is stepping on the brake.

As soon as we have come to a standstill, he nods resolutely. He takes the key out of the ignition and holds up the key chain between his thumb and forefinger.

"If that's the way you want it," he says to the rearview mirror. "You won't interfere with my life and I won't interfere with your life? Fine. Then take care of things yourself too. You drive."

I look at Axel and at the words that come out of his mouth, and after that I look around, at what might be expected there.

My mother is looking wide-eyed at my brother. Her hand, which, with a handkerchief in it, was dabbing at Bordzek's scrape, hovers motionless in the air. Bordzek rubs his temple with a couple of fingers and in this way shields his face from my mother and me.

"I'm stopping here," Axel says again. He points into the distance, in the direction of Bonnie's house. The house is out in front of us, beckoning even, with a cooling fan and cold near beer, but it is still a way to drive, and Axel is not driving there. His hands move apart like sliding doors.

"No," he says.

"Ax," says my mother, and she moves her head forward, in my direction. My brother grins and looks at me.

"Am I maybe saying something that she's not supposed to hear?" he asks my mother.

I lay a hand over Edie's free ear. I feel my eyes grow rigid. They always get that staring look when Axel and my mother start exchanging shots.

Axel is fuming. I can feel it. Deep inside, the lid is off the powder keg again. His hand shoots toward the door handle on his side. The door flies open as if it had no weight, and before I know it, Axel's legs are standing outside and the seat beside me is empty.

My mother sighs. She sighs in a way that can't be imitated. There are half-words in it, and curses, and the question why he is being so aggravating today, this is not the weather to be acting up, he said, didn't he, that nothing mattered to him, and a few more sighs follow.

"Will you wait here?" she says to Bordzek. She would really like to give him a kiss, but she restrains herself. She takes hold of his arm for a second, and he throws a dirty look my way and mumbles, "Idiotka," which is Polish for "sweetheart," ha ha. My mother hushes him and with her other hand she pushes Vlad, who has already figured out that another door is about to be opened, down.

My mother gets out. An army tank rolling out.

I look at Edie, who is looking up at me out of the corner of her eye, and I give her a smile.

"We don't know about anything, Edie," I whisper. "We don't know about anything. Seven times."

Edie shakes her head.

My mother passes by my door. She is looking at the ground, and her hands are fists. She goes over to stand beside my brother, just about the way they were standing before, but this time farther away from the car.

I look at them, at those two people. My mother in her black stretch pants in which her butt cheeks bulge, and over them that T-shirt with the panther on the front. It is a very ugly T-shirt, certainly if my mother hasn't washed her black hair and out of convenience has tied it back in a ponytail. Then the hair fits with the T-shirt as well as the other way around.

My brother doesn't fit with her. His beige pants look good on him, and his shirt, which looks like a lit-up apartment building, fits with the pants. He has chest hair coming up over his open collar, and I know he smells good. Even if he hasn't bathed, he still smells good. Edie has the same thing.

Axel sticks out one hand toward my mother. By the look of him, she's going to have something explained to her, something that hadn't been clearly said before.

Bordzek stares off. His arms lie beside his body. His dog leans against him, hunched over with one leg up in the air, licking where it itches. The sky could fall,

Bordzek wouldn't notice.

All of a sudden Edie stirs. She pushes herself up, her hand in the middle of my chest, and fixes me with her eyes. She poses a question without words, an important question, and I answer her: I shake my head. I know exactly what she's referring to. She is asking about the sounds we hear at night, the two of us, in the room we share, if we're allowed to ask questions about the sounds we hear.

No, I tell her with my eyes, we're not asking any questions. We'll wait until the answer comes by itself. It will come soon, it's coming.

I look around.

Bordzek looks back.

I raise my eyebrows and jerk my head to the side, to indicate that I notice as he does that Axel is talking with my mother and that they're probably talking about Bordzek again, and doesn't that make him nervous?

He looks as if he didn't have to take notice of what I asked. I didn't ask it out loud, so he thinks he can turn his eyes away from me, then come back with a question, also one without words. I think he's asking about the sounds he causes at night. If maybe I know more, if maybe I wake up, if maybe I'm awake?

I would like to answer out loud, but I'm smart. I say nothing. Not No either.

Bordzek's dog stops licking, stands with his front paws beside me, and pants in my direction, his tongue hanging crookedly out of his mouth. It lets off a stench that's impossible to bear.

"*God*, Vlad," I say, and I shove him back with my elbow as I look away from him and Bordzek. I hear his paws slip in between the middle console and the seat and I hear him smack his chin.

Good, I think. I reach my hand up to my forehead, because I am heavy from thinking. I look at the wheat field we are parked beside that's not much to look at, and I shut my eyes for a moment so I don't have to see anything anymore.

At that instant, Edie gently tugs my sleeve.

"I don't feel good," she says.

I open my eyes wide, just from the shock of Edie's

saying something, and I look straight into her face. She looks very pale and her lips are pursed into a point as if she had a bad taste in her mouth.

I push open the door and grab her by her upper arms. I set her outside, a tree I plant in a hole, and duck out after her.

Edie's upper body snaps forward and tosses what she ate this afternoon. This afternoon it was a plate she mashed at with her fork without eating any. Now it turns out to have been a plate of beans in a greenish sauce.

"Oh, sweetie," I sing to her, and I hold her by the shoulders and give them a squeeze, as if more would come. More does come, and I taste in her stead the sourness and shake my head, maybe then I will get rid of the odor in my nose, but no, Edie isn't done by a long shot. She snaps forward and again throws up in an arc into the grass. I see that some of it lands on her dress.

I look for my handkerchief, look around at my mother, could she do her work, help her child, but she is talking with Axel, making big gestures. Evidently she has no time for her youngest daughter, for her youngest daughters. Just let those two puke, she thinks, they're good at that.

"Goddammit, Mother!" I shout all of a sudden.

I believe I do the same thing that Axel did with the car. I drive backward with words, with expletives in my case. The lid to my powder keg flies off all at once, too.

As soon as my mother is standing beside me, breathing in my face, taking Edie over from me, I throw up my hands. I show the sky my hands. I say I've had enough.

"I've had goddamn enough," I say, and I walk off a way into the grass on the side of the road, until I feel that my head must be as red as a buoy, because I am seeing red in front of my eyes as well. I'm swaying on my legs. I tell myself I have to stay in control. These days nobody is in control of themselves anymore. The heat in my head makes it hard. I hope somebody will catch hold of me, I'm going to pass out soon, I can feel it. I can't get enough air. I see dark spots in front of my eyes.

Axel throws his arms around me.

I feel my arms and legs tense up. Everything around falls silent.

My mother is looking at me over her shoulder. She holds Edie by the head with her two hands. Edie gasps for air like a fish. The dear child is staring at me, with spittle on her lips and a couple of beans on her dress, and her little hands move spastically while her chest works up and down fast.

Axel turns on his heel, and I have to turn with him. He takes care that I don't see anybody anymore, Bordzek either, whom I think I see in a flash beside the car. We look in the direction that Axel doesn't want to go, direction Bonnie.

Sweat beads up on my forehead. A drop slides through my eyebrows and falls onto my cheek. My face goes limp. I try not to think of anything else. I lean against Axel more than at first and am not ashamed. Sweat is sweat, and tears are water too.

Axel pulls me closer and offers me his shoulder.

This is the way Edie must feel when she's lying against my neck and smells my hair. Axel smells like his clothes, smells like his room. His breath is warm somewhere near my ear.

"Too much. Right, Sis?" he says to me.

I nod against his neck. "Too much."

I hear him think. For a few seconds, his thoughts dart in all directions. I raise my eyes so I can see his mouth. He is weighing his words. He tries an *o,* he tries an *a,* but in the end he just says what he knows. "Well, you know a lot, Sis."

I smile.

Axel and I ran into each other in the hallway in front of the bathroom door last night. Neither of us is stupid. Fifteen seconds earlier and I would have seen Bordzek's heels as he entered my mother's room. Thirty seconds earlier and I would have seen where he was coming from.

This time I only ran into Axel naked.

An "I'm sorry" is coming, I think, and I'm already shaking my head. He doesn't have to feel sorry. It's my fault. I should be asleep at night. I should just stay in bed. I shouldn't play doll mother with Edie like that, taking care that she goes back to sleep if she has woken up, and then keep sitting on the edge of her bed. I shouldn't stare into the darkness of the room as I hear

Axel sighing in his. I should crawl under the blankets, plug my ears, avoid hearing Bordzek when he crosses the hallway to my mother's room. I shouldn't hear Axel turn on his side, trying to go back to sleep without thinking about what Bordzek did with him.

"I'm not staying at home," Axel says in my ear. "As soon as I can, I'm leaving."

I look at him and expect a sad face, but my brother is smiling.

"You should talk about it with Bonnie," he says. "You know a lot, little sister, but Bonnie knows everything."

He plants a kiss on my nape and then throws his arm around my neck. I have the feeling I can't budge an inch, can't retreat a hair from his body, I am so close to my brother.

"Let me go, Axel," I say. "Let me go."

"Mother knows very well what we're talking about, Sis. I told her again today and again she doesn't believe me. She doesn't want to believe me. I am painting her lover black, she says. I am jealous of her happiness, she says. I'm fantasizing, she says."

"Yes," I say, and I grin. "But be a bit quieter when you fantasize at night."

As if my mother knew that she has come up in our conversation, she starts sounding noisier. She tells Edie a joke and laughs overly loudly at it. Just plain loud would already have been overdone.

Edie stands there as if she peed in her pants. She looks at me. I can see she's waiting for me to come over.

Axel gives me a kiss, on the top of my head this time. That's the way I always do with Edie. I can hear Axel saying that Bonnie will take care of us when he's gone. And otherwise I'd better take care of everybody.

"And of yourself, of course," he says, and I nod, as if I had already freed myself from him and were with Edie.

She stands there so helplessly, with the beans and that green spot still on her chest. Was my mother looking around the whole time so that she didn't even notice that little bit of dirtiness?

I squeeze Axel's arms so he'll know that I am fond of him. I smile up at him so he'll also know that I understand him. After that I let him go. I have to go back to Edie.

She just about leaps into my arms. She stinks to high heaven, but what do I care? I am calm inside and if possible will become calmer because Edie is hugging me to death and is already getting up on my lap although we're not sitting. I almost start singing.

"Momma says most of the argument is over," says Edie.

I am again startled by her little voice, which we get to hear only once in a blue moon.

"That's right," I say. "And all the people are nice, nice, nice again."

"Four more times," says Edie. "Seven times."

I pick her up, hug her, and turn toward the car.

Axel is standing on the driver's side and is looking at us over the rounded roof of the car.

"Are we going to Bonnie's now?" he says to Edie.

"Yes, Bonnie," says Edie.

My mother pretends to smile. She looks over the top of the car at Bordzek, who is just getting in. She also tries smiling some more underneath the roof, but she still gets no response, and after a while Axel interrupts her. He says Edie can sit in front, because that's how we left, didn't we?

"And nobody objects to that, right?"

No, nobody objects to that.

My mother wants to slide over on the back seat so that she can sit beside Bordzek, with Vlad on her lap, maybe, who knows, but Axel sticks his arm in and makes a little clucking sound with his tongue. He dangles the key chain in front of my mother's face.

"As agreed," he says.

"Oh?" says my mother. "Did we agree on that?"

"Yes," says Axel. "But we can also go on foot."

My mother grins, even though there's a rancid edge to it, and works her way out. She walks around the car, snatches the keys that Axel demonstratively holds up for her as she goes by, and sits down with a sigh. Again the sigh couldn't be imitated. A word and a curse and a groaning question.

I shake my head and slide in beside Bordzek. I can only think that my mother is acting like a baby. These days nobody, really nobody, can control themselves anymore.

Axel squeezes in beside me on the back seat. He takes up less space than my mother did. I can breathe better. His butt is warm in a nicer way, too.

He holds his back and head straight as he's looking at me from the side and grins broadly. He is waiting for me to hold his hand. I will hold his hand, but first I still have to get used to a few thoughts. I smile with lips curled out.

"Damn," says my mother, because she can't find the ignition right away.

"Seven times," says Edie.

"Not always," I say.

Still my mother continues to swear. Almost seven times, until we leave. The car moves haltingly, then drives up the hill.

It's not far to Bonnie's house anymore. The red roof is already getting a lot redder.

Soon there will be cake. Soon we'll be sitting with ice-cold near beer under a secondhand fan that throbs like a helicopter.

I hope Bonnie will say blunt things. "Who nailed

their faces shut? Why aren't those two turtledoves cooing?"

"Because they're thinking things over, Bonnie," I'll be able to say, calmer than she is, so that I can feel older than I am.

I look to my left, at Bordzek. He sags against the car door and is staring at the inside of his hat, which is lying on his lap. Vlad's head is lying on his knee. The animal finally has its eyes shut.

The wheat fields seem to be gliding underneath us.

I look the other way, at where Axel is sitting, looking at me with amusement. I should make a face at him, but I don't feel like it, so I don't.

I would prefer to keep looking into the rearview mirror until the end of the trip, at my mother's dark eyes.

Her eyelashes are black, her eyebrows are black, her eyelids glisten with sweat. Her skin is pink. She is squinting her eyes a little bit against the light, but she still looks as if it were raining outside.

I can hear her swear.

Edie hears it too. She looks sideways and says,

"Seven times goddammit. Seven times, that brings good luck, Momma."

The passenger seat squeaks. Edie peers over the top of the seat. Since she saw her beans again, she seems to have woken up. She looks at Bordzek and she looks at Axel, as if she were comparing the two, and again she says, "Seven times, that brings good luck. Bordzek knocks seven times too, doesn't he, Axel?"

She pretends the back of the seat is a door, knocks on it seven times, rhythmically, the way Bordzek does, then turns around with a grin. She looks sideways at my mother and slowly lets herself slide down on her bottom.

Axel and I see my mother's face change. She frowns, blinks her eyes, and looks sideways, at Edie, as if she only now heard that Edie said something.

"What did you say, dear?" she says. After that, she almost misses the curve.

Boatman's Arrival

The news arrives in the morning mail. Oh my, looky here at what fell on the mat. We bow our heads with the letter in our hands, read that my mother's mother is dead, and have doubts about our feelings. We are distracted by the wind outside where the leaves are blowing off the trees, and we continue, like my mother, to eat breakfast.

We are inheriting money. We are also allowed to choose furniture and stuff if we want. My brother thinks of junk, like the clock he looked at when he was four and he was staying over at my mother's mother's and did nothing but long for home. Myself, I think of jewelry, or at least of an old watch with a photo of my mother's father under the cover. I never saw it before in my life though. My little sister is sitting on the cabinet where she loves to sit, folding boats. She is not curious about things. She waits as we do for the living part.

To our surprise, my mother's mother also left behind a person. It is a man, we think. We have received a name, Skip the Boatman, which we think is a funny name that sounds boyish.

Still, Skip the Boatman has to be a man. During our grandmother's last days, he supposedly cooked for and took care of her, and a boy our age can't do that, says Axel. I say boys can cook and care for people, because Axel wants to hear that, but I am thinking, as he is, of a grown-up man.

We are looking forward to his arrival. He will bring a few things when he comes, as much as he can carry, and he will also bring himself, because it has been decided that he will come to live with us for a time.

My mother's mother mentioned nothing about time in her last will and testament. There is only a question: whether the stranger, whom she always called Skip the Boatman because he likes that, can stay with us for as long as it takes.

A request in a will is a law. You have to give dead people what they ask, certainly if you get money for it in return.

My mother's mother never gave us anything when she was alive. No money, no property, no love.

"But that's history," says Axel. "What's important is that on her deathbed she realized that we missed out on a number of things."

My mother thinks that we should go to a monastery, that we will be declared saints—that's how good she thinks we are. If it were up to her, she would put Skip the Boatman on a raft with no food and shove him off, away from the shore. "I never heard about him before, and I had nothing but trouble with her."

Axel and I keep our mouths shut. Edie, too. If Bonnie were here, she would set my mother straight. Bonnie is the oldest. She's allowed to do that. She does that when Mother gets too crude.

Axel and I are silent and make room for Boatman in the little sewing room on the in-between level. My mother said that somewhere under the boxes there's a fold-out bed. We find it at the end of the morning and fold it out.

It takes us hours, not because the bed is so well hidden and we almost can't find it, but because Axel and I start digging through the boxes.

At first we laugh at what we find, but not after that. The boxes contain memories of my mother's men, and here and there also something of my father's. We go through all the albums that date from before my sister Bonnie was born up until last year. Particularly Axel is silenced by it, certainly when we see how our father goes farther and farther away into the background, finally disappearing entirely from the photographs. Before we know it, we are talking about love, which we don't understand. It's as if we had to make room in our heads as well.

When we are done, we open the window to let in the wind.

My mother says Boatman should be happy. He has a bed with its own bedspread, and out of the boxes and a board, Axel and I made a writing table for him at the window. He can sit and write if he can write. It's a bit of a squeeze for the chair between the bed and the closet, so we hope he is thin and wiry. We pushed my mother's old clothes all the way to the side of the closet and wrapped them in a wide skirt. That way he can put his clothes away.

"We did a good job," says Axel. "Now, if you make him a drawing, Sis, he'll feel completely welcome."

I can draw well. Axel always says that a person who can draw well has two qualities at once. People who are good at drawing look closely and see more.

After dinner I start on it. I already know at the table what I'm going to draw because my mother tells about how it used to be, about the slipshod household she grew up in. She also talks a long time about her dead mother. About how men could never stand being with her for more than six months, and that it was a miracle that this Mr. Boatman stayed with her until her last breath.

"*Skip* the Boatman," says Axel. "*Skip* the Boatman must be a very good and patient man."

"A golden man, really," I say.

"I couldn't care less," says my mother. "He was able

to stand being with her for a long time, that's the only thing I know and think is odd. Nothing but good things about the dead. Except, I don't really know what to say about my mother."

Boatman must have beautiful thoughts when he sees the drawing.

To the left, I draw our grandmother's house as I know it from pictures. To the right, there is a table with a cloth on it. Then I draw my mother's mother and Skip the Boatman himself, both seen from the back because I don't know what they look like from the front. My grandmother and Skip are drinking red wine. Red is for love. The wine is festive. I work for a long time coloring.

The hardest are the letters. I put them at the top of the drawing in different colors—Welcome Skip the Boatman—and then the drawing is done. It has to go up on the front door, over the little window, so tonight light will shine through it from inside. It will look welcoming.

I can picture it, Skip who feels welcome because of my lit-up drawing with the name he likes to hear written above it. But luck isn't really on my side.

The sky grows dark when Edie and Axel and I are sweeping the path to the front door. We don't even have time to run inside with dry hair. From one minute to the next, it starts pouring, leaden drops. They make the yard and the house throb like a drum.

Axel and I stand breathing hard inside on the mat. Axel says, "Now the path will be clean for sure," and at first I have to giggle, but then I choke because of what I see. My drawing is getting wet.

Axel sees me looking at the little window in the front door. From inside, you can see how the colors are running. It almost makes me cry. All my work was work for nothing.

My mother, who wants to know why we're standing there doing nothing, comforts me. She says that I don't have to mop the kitchen floor, that she'll do it. She says, "Go peel potatoes for tonight, you're good at that. And you, Axel, help me mop. We'll hang up a couple of garlands instead of that drawing. Edie'll climb up to the attic, she thinks those narrow stairs are such a thrill, and she can go look for those old ones with the stars, that's more than enough. Come on, Edie, we'll go look for them. We're not going to act like the king is coming." She waves her hand beside her face as if she were throwing air over her shoulder.

I hope that Skip will still feel welcome now that my drawing has run and there will soon be old garlands in the hallway. I walk into the kitchen behind Axel and fill a bucket with water while Axel picks out the nicest-looking potatoes for me. I'm suddenly almost happy. I tell him so, too. Axel says that he understands what I mean.

"Skip will change something around here," he says. "Mark my words. We're going to get a father who's decent."

I bite my lip.

Upstairs, my mother jumps for the attic trapdoor. We hear her say something to Edie. The fold-down stairs squeak. It seems as if the sound of the rain were falling out of the hole to the attic. The tapping on the roof tiles can be heard down in the kitchen. It's a cozy sound.

I get a glass of water, I'm thirsty, and sit down at the table to peel, with my feet up so that Axel can reach everything. He empties the bucket on the floor. The suds smell nice. I feel so good that I simply say, "I hope he's handsome."

Axel doesn't look up. He mops under the table and says that men are dangerous anyway, handsome or not. He says it under his breath. "Or did you forget about last year?"

"I can see him in front of me," I say with a Polish accent, and I pull up my upper lip. "I see him as if he had been here yesterday." It takes me a potato before I dare say anything more about last year. "I'll never forget him."

But then, last year is already history too.

Axel lets the mop drop into the bucket and looks right at me as he straightens up. He smiles.

"In any case, the beginning is already different," he says.

"Yes," I say. "In any case, the beginning is already different."

Axel straightens his back, hesitates for a moment, and then with a simple movement sweeps my glass of water off the table. It smashes to bits on the tiles.

"We still had to break a glass," he says. "For good luck."

The house is all clean when my mother and I are both standing in the decorated front hallway putting on our coats.

Axel and Edie are looking at us from the kitchen. Axel tries to smile, but I can see that he wants to go with us. That's impossible because my mother thinks that we can't all go to the station, and in any event, Edie can't stay home alone.

"Next time we'll toss again, Axel, and then it'll be heads, I know for sure," I say. "Stay inside. You can never tell, Boatman might call. Who knows, maybe you'll be the first one to hear his voice."

This idea appeals to Axel. He sits up straight.

"I don't mind," he says, and he pulls Edie up on his lap. "We'll take care of the house. Bonnie will be by soon, and then you'll be coming back, and in the meantime we'll start cooking."

I nod with satisfaction. I say we won't be gone long. The station isn't far.

"We'll be back in less than an hour. With him." I speak of Skip the Boatman as if I already knew him, and I look that way too.

My mother and I blow Axel and Edie a kiss through the air, and then my mother forces me out the door. The rain blows into my face. My mother has an umbrella. I don't. But she gets wet just the same. An umbrella in this foul weather is like sheltering under a newspaper.

I turn up my collar against the cold wind and button the pinching button under my chin. As always, my mother has no patience. I just manage to call out, "Wait for me!" but my voice blows away, or else Momma is pretending she doesn't hear me—she does that a lot.

After a while I've caught her rhythm and we walk in step. Down the path behind the houses near the railroad tracks, across the little bridge, under the soccer field stands where it is dry, away from the houses.

When we reach the straight path between the fields, the fight starts for real. The wind is happy we are there. It is coming from the north and pierces our clothing. I stay close to my mother so we make headway faster.

Every time the umbrella snaps inside out, I help her wrestle with the stays.

All the way to the station we don't say a word. We are not thinking of the same thing. I would dare to bet my life on it. My mother looks angry the whole time, as if there were starch in her eyebrows and nothing could be ironed out.

I'm thinking of Skip the Boatman. I am burning with curiosity inside: about what he looks like, about what his voice sounds like, and about what he brought with him.

I don't know how long we march. I don't pay attention to that, the wind keeps interfering. The trees along the road are almost bare. They whistle, and every gate that is loose bangs open and shut.

I am relieved when I see the station in the distance. The little square in front is empty. In the bicycles racks, there is one bicycle that rocks back and forth and squeaks.

My mother wants to run the last stretch. Is it that we're late, I ask, but then I feel the wind at my back and I understand why she wants to run. We blow toward the station, both giggling, with the umbrella for a sail. We blow into the station making quite a racket. The door slams shut by itself behind us. We both lean against it, and I giggle hard.

"Oo," says my mother. Her umbrella clatters on the stone floor. It makes so much noise that we immediately realize how quiet it is in the station. On the other side, a woman and a boy are sitting on a bench. They are both looking at us. The boy's jacket rustles when he moves. The man behind the ticket window is looking too. He shakes his head—we could tone it down. Startled, we hold our breath.

It becomes as quiet as at the table when somebody has said something wrong.

Above our heads, the station clock ticks. The bicycle outside squeaks.

"Pick it up," my mother whispers to me as she points at the umbrella. Her face is stern. She is always the oldest.

I pick up her umbrella and say, "Oo!" to the puddle growing under our feet. We are still dripping. If we don't take our coats off quickly, we'll have to mop the whole place.

My mother leaves wet footprints behind, up to the bench across from the ticket window. She sits down the minute I look up.

I am standing by myself at the door, and all of a sudden the puddle appears to be all my fault. I make a face at the man behind the ticket window.

"Nasty weather," I say.

My mother says I have to be quiet because she is thinking. She compares the clock with the sign above the ticket window. After a while she nods with satisfaction.

"We got here well in time," I say for her, but she doesn't respond.

Just be quiet, that's what she means.

I look at the clock and think of my grandmother, whom I never saw, and of last year, and finally of Boatman too. When that thought comes up, I startle myself, because I can feel that you could hang the wash out on my smile, that's how broadly I'm grinning.

Skip, I imagine, has the most beautiful sideburns we

have ever seen. He makes us all happy because he has cash in his pockets, bills we're allowed to buy things with, and he enchants us all. He speaks in sentences that come from books, and any clothes look good on him. My mother really wants him to stay because he is kind to her, and she is in love with him and his money and his sentences, and that's fun, since because of that we finally get a happy mother and a father who is decent.

My mother nudges me. "What are you grinning about?" she whispers.

"You don't want to know, Mother," I say, and I grin even more broadly.

"Yes I do, I'm asking," she says. "What are you grinning about?"

"Oh, Momma," I say. "I'm imagining that Skip the Boatman has cash in his pockets." I look at my mother's face, how quickly it will change. "Bills. I imagine that he is kind and has the most beautiful voice in the whole world and sideburns that look awesome on him!"

My mother draws back with a start. She stares straight at me and thinks for a long time. Her face changes, as I expect, but it mostly gets darker. She pulls me down by my arm, lays one leg over the other, and says, "Stupid girl."

I sit down, straight like my mother.

"Stupid girl?" I say.

"Stupid girl," says my mother. "This Mr. Boatman may be handsome or rich or made of gold or all of those things at once, but he comes from my mother, and that already makes him worth a lot less. Anyway, I learned my lesson. I'll grow old by myself."

"Hmm," I go, and with that I want to say that love is rude and indecent and bursts into the coldest houses, because with words like these Axel spoke about love this morning in the sewing room.

My mother shakes her head and points with her chin at the woman and the boy on the other bench. The two of them are gawking at us and would be very curious about all that love dares, if I were to start in on it.

"Shut your mouth," says my mother.

It grows quiet in the station. The rain taps against the windows. The boy on the bench has a cold and can't get any air through his nose. I have to look at him the whole time to see how long he'll keep it up.

My mother nudges me. "Don't gawk at him like that," she says between her teeth. She gets up and walks away from me. I know why she is doing that. She is ashamed of me. For a couple of minutes, she hates me.

I look at the hands of the clock until the man behind the ticket window scrapes his chair and puts on his cap. He acts busy with closet doors and doors to little rooms, and finally comes out into the waiting area by way of a glass cubicle, wearing a long coat. The train is coming, he says to the woman and the boy. They follow him up to the door to the platform. They back away from the damp chill that blows in.

"Wait here," says the woman.

"Wait here," my mother says to me.

We stop some feet from the door. My mother turns toward me to make my wet hair presentable and to ask if she looks presentable.

"The first impression is everything," she says.

"You're fine, Mother," I say. At the same time it occurs

to me that she wants to be pretty for a man whom she already detests beforehand. Anyway, wasn't she going to grow old by herself, even if he was handsome or rich or made of gold or all those things at once?

All of a sudden her raincoat is a coat with a fur collar. Her wet hair shines and glitters as if it were a style that's supposed to look like that. Maybe she has been thinking about the man who is good and patient—so good and patient that he was able to stand being with a piece of work like her mother till her last breath.

I give my mother a shove with my shoulder, so that she inadvertently takes a step forward. Boatman has to see my mother first—the first impression is everything—and if he sees me, his idea will already be formed. He will think: that's a nice woman, and uh ... that has to be her daughter. I know that I'm not pretty but that I get pretty from what's around me.

The windows start to shake as if far away a couple of horses gone berserk were coming our way. All kinds of things are buzzing and singing outside.

Through the window I see the man from the ticket

window pass by. He is holding the top of his cap and walking backward. The train catches up with him. First the locomotive glides by and then come the lit-up windows.

The woman and the boy throw the door open. The noise of the engine blows in with the wind, the noise of hissing doors, of men who laugh loudly.

I close my eyes. I can't take waiting. I am patient if I have to wait for a smile I know. I don't know if Skip ever laughs. I can see only a whole lot of men in front of me, one after another, probably all the men I've ever seen in my life and whose faces I have accidentally remembered.

People enter the station. I don't look, but I hear their voices, feel the cold that they bring with them, can smell if they've smoked. The last man I see in my imagination is Skip the Boatman the way I dream he looks, and I hope that in real life he has blond hair that glows. I don't want to be disappointed when I open my eyes. If he disappoints me, I won't let on. No, I'll smooth my face the way my mother always does.

At that moment of all moments, my mother says beside me, "That isn't him, is it?"

I open my eyes.

Down the platform walks a man who has turned up the collar of his coat. Through the window we see the top of his body. He appears to be dragging something heavy. It is even making the muscles in his face pull. He puts down the thing we can't see, looks around at it once, then makes his way back to where he came from, onto the train.

My mother looks at me. "A sailor," she says. "I should have known. Of course he's a sailor. And a shady one, by the look of it."

I nod. She is right. I saw the yellow brass buttons on his coat too. Sailors have yellow brass buttons on their overcoats. The shadiness I didn't notice.

"Nobody said anything about a sailor," I say.

"Nobody said anything about anything," says my mother.

We are both startled by the loud warning whistle. My mother takes a few steps toward the door, as if she would like to hold the train back. She looks as I do in surprise at the lit-up windows that start to move, glide by, speed up. There are only a few, so before we are really aware of it the last window shoots past us, and the noise of the train ebbs away into the distance.

What stays behind is the drone of the rain, the dripping on the vaulted roof over the platform. My idea of meeting Skip the Boatman had been different.

"Are you sure it was this train?" I ask.

"I can tell time," says my mother.

On time Skip is not, in any case. He should have been standing there already, there in front of us, smiling, in his coat, with sailor's buttons if need be. The open doorway is causing a noisy draft, with the empty platform behind it, the wildly swaying trees behind that, and still farther away, the first darkness.

"This is not possible," I say.

The stationmaster is looking at something on the ground.

My mother sees what the man is doing and walks toward the door. She looks around the corner. She is taken aback. I imagine that Skip is there beside the door lying on top of his suitcases. Loaded. We're taking in a drunk, unwashed sailor.

I have just enough time to think: don't let it be true, or soon she'll be in love again with something that isn't decent. My mother calls over her shoulder that I have to come help carry suitcases. I can see that she is bending forward, walking farther down the platform toward something that is smaller than herself. I also walk bending forward, because I want to see Skip lying on top of his suitcases as quickly as possible. I'm sick of the excitement and can't look around the corner quickly enough. Then when I am finally at that point, am prepared for the worst, and look, I am not face to face with a small man. I don't see a big man sprawled on his back. My mother and I are surrounded by suitcases and chests and bags with our name stuck on them. And in the middle of it all, like a bicycle with a mountain of blankets on top of it, is a wheelchair with an old man in it, the thinnest man I have ever seen in my life.

My mother chokes back a curse. She holds on to her cheek and with her other hand she holds on to her mouth, and she looks from Boatman to the stationmaster, shaking her head.

"Is this for us?" she says.

The stationmaster looks around as if he had to make sure of it himself. "Yes," he says, pointing at a label. "Isn't that your name?"

"You're joking," says my mother. "You're joking." She plants her two hands in the air and moves them back and forth while she turns her eyes so that she doesn't have to look at Boatman anymore. "Tell me it's a joke."

"I'm afraid not," replies the stationmaster.

"Ha?" says my mother. She pretends to laugh and shakes her shoulders loose. "I'm afraid not. I'm afraid I'm going to leave everything where it is." She wipes a wet strand from her forehead. "Now *that* would be a joke."

"Momma, just say hello to Boatman first," I say with a nod at the wheelchair.

I do what I can to smile, but my face is too tense. I am not able to hide my disappointment as well as I thought. There's no time for me to get used to the way Boatman is sitting there, either. He is not a sailor, not a young man, not a handsome man. He is an old, almost dead man.

Now and then he moves his lips as if he were chewing on his tongue, and then I hear that he is mumbling something. What he is saying I don't understand.

"Later," my mother says to me, and she turns away from the wheelchair. She searches in her purse. First I think she wants to blow her nose or is just doing something to avoid Boatman, but I see that she is taking out money. She allows a bill to be seen between two fingers, steps over a package and a bag, and tucks it into the stationmaster's pocket.

"The address is right," she says as she points her little finger down at the chest at her feet that has a label on it with our particulars.

"But...," says the man.

"Yessir, you're bringing everything to our house," says my mother, and with her eyes she shoves the rest of his sentence back into his mouth. She gives him a smile he can't resist.

That smile doesn't stay stuck for long. Her eyebrows slide back into place, her cheeks hang down, her head drops forward, she lets her arms sag. All of a sudden she picks up her foot as if she had felt fire, and she sings out, "What's *that?*"

The stationmaster spreads his arms.

"A dog," he says.

"Yes," says Boatman.

"Oh, no," I say.

I bend over toward the wooden crate that scared my mother. It has holes in it and heat is pouring out of them and there is a sound coming out of an animal that is panting and whining too, if you listen closely.

Not again, I think. Last year we already had a dog. This one better have some meat on its rump.

My mother doesn't hope for anything anymore. She holds the nail of her index finger against her lips and decides that she doesn't want to see what she has to see. She's good at that. She turns on her heel, makes a beckoning little sound between her tongue and her teeth, and says, "Hokay," as if I were the dog. She expects that I will follow her, straight through the station.

I won't do it. We have a guest. I follow her up to the

door and there I say, "And Skip?" My voice echoes. The station is so empty that I seem to be shouting. "You're forgetting Skip."

"I'm not forgetting Skip," my mother retorts louder than necessary because she is annoyed by me and wants to make fun of me. She jerks the door outside open and again turns around, the door latch in her hand. She is incredibly annoyed by me, I can see that from the way she slaps her forehead, and she is annoyed by the squeaking of the door, I notice that from the way she holds her arm. She is also annoyed by the light inside, by the wind at her back, by the twilight outside, by the lone bicycle rocking back and forth.

"You push his chair," she says, still too loudly. "Otherwise he won't find the way."

"They," I say. "Otherwise *they* won't find the way."

I turn around, walk back to Boatman, want to ask him what the name of his dog is, but he is looking at me from his chair, and from looking comes staring, and from staring he gets glassy eyes.

"Take him with you," says the stationmaster as he

lays his hand on my back and forces me in the direction of the wheelchair. "Don't worry about the dog. I'll bring it to the house along with the packages and the bags. You just take care of your grandfather."

"Yes," I say, and right after that I want to correct myself. "No!" But there's no need anymore. Boatman has become my grandfather, which isn't all that bad. It's very comforting, in fact. I believe I already know his movements. He is making kneading motions with his hands again now, as if there were dough in his lap.

"Hokay," I say to Boatman, but not the way my mother would say it. I shove a few packages aside, wheel him down the platform, and bend over his shoulder.

"Is there something I should be thinking about?" I say to him.

"Huh?" he goes, and he holds his gnarled hand up like a shell, much too far away from his ear.

"If there's something I should be thinking about."

He bows his head and grins. "No." And he mumbles something again.

I am already halfway down the waiting area when I

understand that he is saying that I should think about whatever I like to think about. As long as it's something pleasant. He mentions a color, a smell, the sky. It is not the answer I expected, because I wanted to know if I had to pay attention to something in particular, but I'm already thinking of the color red, and of a smell—that of the rain now—and of the gray sky, and I startle myself, because I believe that Boatman's head resembles mine.

"Stupid girl!" I whisper to myself.

"Yes!" he says, but he couldn't have heard me.

"Now I'm thinking of my little sister," I say with my mouth right near the back of his ear. "And of your warm bed. And of your warm dinner that's ready and waiting."

I turn the chair so I can open the door. I saw through the window that my mother is fit to burst with annoyance. It would be best if she didn't let any words come out of her mouth, because she will make a curse of "Welcome!" and "We're happy you're here," she will morph into an expletive and a few complaints.

As soon as I start wheeling the chair outside, she makes it clear she is to march off briskly. In less than no time she has crossed the little square. She makes butting motions with her head because her wet collar is getting in her way. She doesn't avoid a single puddle. She steps into one and walks straight through another. Sometimes the mud spatters on her legs. She stands and waits on the other side, in the shelter of a bicycle stall.

"That's my mother," I say into the wind.

Boatman mumbles. I don't think he heard me.

I push the wheelchair over the threshold and try to catch up to my mother, or no, keep up with her, because she is already setting off at a rapid pace. My hands grip the handlebars, my arms are rigid from the strain. I push against the chair as if there were only one single direction. Straight ahead.

"Mother," I say, when I am right near her.

"Save your comments!" she says over her shoulder. She waves me away with her hand. "Don't predict anything, don't begin fantasizing. The only thing I want to imagine is that I'm already home and wearing dry clothes."

"You don't know what I'm going to say, Mother."

"And I don't have to know either." She sticks her umbrella out in front of herself, shakes it, pushes it open, and throws it up in a single motion so that all of a sudden it is up over her head like a big hat. The wind picks it up and in a second snaps it inside out.

"Mother," I say emphatically. "At least say something to Boatman."

She continues to walk, snaps her umbrella shut, doesn't turn around.

I look at my mother's back. I wait for the moment that she will stand still and turn around and act happy. She knows the way she's supposed to be polite to new people, doesn't she? Open your arms and act happy. She doesn't even really have to be happy.

She stands still, but she doesn't say anything, and she doesn't do anything. Acting as if it is also too much to ask. Her eyes are shut. She pushes her thumb and index finger against the bridge of her nose. She is looking for words somewhere in the pain in her brain.

Skip and I get a few feet past her.

Finally she says something to my back. She says it

quietly. "A bed, but attention is too much to ask. A bed, that's all he gets."

I let go of the chair and take half a step toward my mother.

"He's not staying forever," I whisper.

My mother wants time to think and therefore snaps open her umbrella again. She raises it a few inches. She wants to see my face. As soon as she sees the way my face looks, she shakes her head.

"He's not staying forever," she says. "Don't you see he's old? My mother saddled us with an old man." She sighs deeply.

"In her will, it said that he was to stay," I say. "But: for as long as it takes. That's what it said."

"Believe what you want, my dear. Boatman will transform into a young sailor yet tonight. Of course. He'll become twenty-one, stay over, and leave again when the sea calls. Of course, of course, believe what you want." She shrugs her shoulders, asks the sky how it is possible that I was ever born, and walks past me.

"You and your sailor," I say. "Boatman's not a sailor.

Nobody said anything about a sailor." She is dreaming about a sailor, that must be it.

My throat feels thick from all the words that I swallow. I have to pinch my mouth shut, brace my feet. My heart goes crazy under my raincoat.

"You always think of yourself first," I blurt out before my mother gets too far away.

Level with Boatman, she stops. She heard me, but she's not sure *what* she heard.

"I said, you always think of yourself first," I say again, louder. "We want everything for you. We do everything to please you. We're fed up with suitcases too, were long ago. We'd have liked not to have anybody, or else the kind of father who would stay for a long time for once. But now that it's Boatman, I think it's fine too. Finally peace and quiet from a man who wants nothing."

I shove my hands deep down into my pockets, hide my head between my shoulders. Touch me and I'll lash out. I could say something else about my mother's mother, that my mother maybe resembles her mother more than she'd like, but that, too, I swallow.

I walk around the wheelchair, straighten Boatman's coat over his legs, and give him a smile. Then I return to my place behind the handlebars. I push the wheelchair with all my might onto the side of the path. It's easier to walk there than through the puddles and the patches of mud on the path, because the grass is short.

My mother follows. She hesitates more than she walks. I can see that over my shoulder.

I march on. With a little speed, the pushing is easier. I have to keep it up. Not think about my mother, who could, for instance, lend us her umbrella. I have to march on. Up ahead there is a stretch of gravel. Wheeling will demand even less effort there, and under the soccer stands the ground will be hard too.

Skip the Boatman mumbles something again, but what he says means nothing. At least, I think it means nothing.

"Wait!" my mother calls out all of a sudden.

I walk on. Under my coat it's steaming. My arms hurt, my knees are shaking from the effort. We're almost home. "Now I'm thinking about my brother and my oldest sister," I call out against the back of Skip's ear. "They will be happy to see you."

The rain lashes at my face. I have to huddle in my coat. The wind whistles around the stands and blows hard. It almost cuts. I shiver and turn my face away.

"Wait!" my mother calls out again.

Behind my back she is struggling with her umbrella, but she keeps on walking. I can't walk fast with a wheelchair though, and maybe I hold back my steps for a few seconds. She gets the chance to catch up with me.

Of course she still has to act testy at first. Couldn't I have waited for her in the first place? What she does then is the opposite of the way she sounds. She says "Damn" one more time, then takes my arm as if she were a friend of mine. She pretends to help push the wheelchair with one hand and looks at me.

"What's wrong with that?" she says, before I can ask.

"What's wrong with that?" I repeat.

"Nothing," she says.

All of a sudden she acts as if it were a summer evening. We are wet under our coats, but in her head she is dry as she walks across the little bridge. Later she will tell me what's wrong with that. Or tomorrow, maybe.

We follow the path behind the houses near the railroad tracks and look inside people's homes. All the pretty kitchen lamps are on. Everybody is sitting under them.

"It's better this way," says my mother all of a sudden.

I think I'll have to give that one remark a lot of thought. In my opinion, my mother means I'm right.

She makes us stand still and lays her arm over my shoulder. It's better this way. Again she doesn't say more. I have to guess the rest or make it up myself.

I say, "Look. Our house is the warmest."

It's true. Our house radiates light. Light falls out of all the windows. It's easy to tell from our whole house in which way the rain is falling.

"I think," I say.

"You think too much," says my mother.

I shake her arm so she can see what I think. "I think that Bonnie and Axel and Edie will be happy," I say. "Don't you think so?"

We stand still at the same time and turn our heads

until we find the best direction for our best ear and hear the song far away behind the sound of the rain. Bonnie and Axel and Edie are singing to pass the time. I recognize the melody from one of the old records Axel collects and recognize their voices. I know that Edie growls when she sings. I almost know for sure that they are waiting in our kitchen.

My mother makes a sound with her tongue. She looks disapproving, but the corners of her mouth curl up. "He is expected!" she says.

"You are expected," I say to Boatman's ear and I tug my mother along by the arm.

We are still walking like girlfriends, but then, separate from each other too. Now and then we bump into each other. We keep trying to walk faster. What binds us is the wheelchair that we are both holding on to.

Bonnie's and Axel's and Edie's voices move more and more clearly around our house.

My mother looks for her key. They won't hear the doorbell inside.

She looks along with me at my forgotten drawing in

front of the window. Two blotchy people with blotchy glasses of red wine. She chuckles and gives the door a little push.

"Here we are, Mr. Boatman," she says.

Inside they are singing.

My mother smiles. We both catch a glimpse of Bonnie in the kitchen, with her mouth open and her arms held out, singing la-la-la, and push Boatman inside. We hold each other up. We could be convulsing with laughter, because Bonnie and Axel and Edie sing so awfully, but we end up grinning in the doorway.

In front of us lies the lit-up kitchen. It has never been so bright.

Bonnie has a glass of wine in her hand and is singing with her eyes shut. Axel is singing to himself, sitting on the arm of a chair, his arms around himself. He is looking at Edie, sitting with her rearend on the table, but he doesn't really see her. In his head he is a singer in an auditorium.

Edie is looking at him and does see him. She dangles her legs over the edge, enjoying herself. She looks from

Bonnie to Axel and back and sings along in her own way.

She isn't startled when she catches sight of us. Her mouth just snaps into a broad grin. She throws her hands up and cries, "There he is!"

She looks as if she had known Boatman for years already and he looks at her that way too, as if he had always fit in this kitchen. Almost a hundred years already, or since the wheelchair has been in existence.

Boatman sits up in his wheelchair and wants to show that he is older and more crooked than a grandfather can ever get. He also wants to let this be heard. He doesn't need a beat. He promptly yammers along with what Bonnie and Axel and Edie start singing.

Axel's jaw drops. Bonnie's chest shakes with laughter. They both try to keep singing but they can't manage very well. Only Boatman and Edie keep up the beat.

I pull on my mother's sleeve and point at Skip with my chin. Does my mother see his old hands, his leathery skin, the wrinkled bags under his eyes?

I whisper in her ear, "He won't stay long, Mother!"

"No," she says. She seeks a spot right by my ear for

her mouth. “No, he won’t stay long.”

The glass of grenadine beside Edie is shaking back and forth.

I predict. Soon there will be more broken glass.

What Are They Doing Over There in Charlestown?

They don't sleep back to back. They sleep side by side, or stomach to back, like anybody would. They sleep together. They only have one bed.

The air in their house has been stagnant the whole week already. Nothing helps. The windows are open for the breeze, but inside the air stays thick and hot. The water from the faucet is already lukewarm, too.

My brother and his Mortimer could sleep outside, under their piece of the open sky, but they don't. Outside, it's swarming with bumblebees as soon as the sun comes up. Starting at five-thirty, it begins to hum and buzz out there in their yard, and that's early. My brother and Mortimer should know that they won't be bothered by the bumblebees. If they were to sleep outside and lie like spoons, they would hear only each other's breath.

At this moment, they are talking about what they already unpacked and about what they still have to unpack. They are sitting together out on their seven-by-twenty-five-foot patio. They are eating something cold and quick because they are tired and because they are hot from working. They feel they have earned white wine. From a house farther down comes the sound of music. A man is singing along, although he doesn't sing loudly. The sky is blue with a lot of light in it, as if something of the day were still lingering there.

My brother lifts his head, looks in the direction of his right ear, as if he could hear me in the distance. He misses me. He misses his sis. His gaze slips over to the other side of the table, and he says to Mortimer, who is draped languidly in a lawn chair, that he's not altogether happy without me.

No, he doesn't say that.

"I'm tired." That's what he says.

The music stops in the middle of a chord. Somewhere, with a lot of noise, a window is slammed shut. It suddenly gets so quiet in Charlestown that my brother and Mortimer don't dare talk anymore. They get up and stack the dishes and glasses. They fold up their lawn chairs. My brother looks at the sky once more before he goes inside. After that, another day has passed. The night begins.

Mortimer falls asleep quickly, but Axel thinks things over for a long time. He thinks of me. He tries his left side, his back, his right side, he churns the sheet loose, thinks of home and particularly of me. He sees me sitting in the kitchen, across from Bonnie at the big table. His picture of Bonnie is spotty. He has studied her too little to really remember at this point what she looks like. But then, it has been only since last week that she has been coming to take care of Edie and Boatman and me while my mother's not around once again. If my brother wants to see me, he only has to close his eyes. He closes his eyes a whole lot.

He would like to know where I am and what I'm thinking. At this moment, for example, he is looking over my shoulder at my hands, which I have laid on the table in front of me. He is looking at my recently chewed-down nails, at the loose bits of skin and the blood here and there, and lays his hands over them. He says in my ear that I can't be eating myself.

I turn my hands over, let my fingers slide between his, and hold his hands. I wouldn't mind if I had to sit like that for an hour. I look at Bonnie on the other side of the table, settle myself against my brother in my thoughts, and make sure that he hears what I say to Bonnie.

"What are you knitting that for anyway?"

Bonnie looks up. The light from the lamp above the table falls halfway down her face.

"Just, you know," she says.

She sits and looks for a while at the baby sock on her knitting needle. I look at it as well. My brother looks too.

"For when you have kids?" I say.

"No, uh-uh," says Bonnie. "For nobody in particular. For somebody someday who's had a baby. I don't know, haven't thought about it yet." She toys with a little sound in her mouth.

"Not for you?" I say. My brother nudges me. "I mean," I say, "you should start thinking about kids, shouldn't you?"

"Should, should," says Bonnie. "There's nothing I have to do. Tomorrow I have to work, sure, and these days I've got my hands full with you guys."

Bonnie looks over in the direction of the kitchen door. My thoughts dart in the same direction, to Boatman, who is old and has trouble thinking things over.

We put him outside, on the path to the gate near the little road that runs along the yards, because that is where he likes to sit the most.

He is old, really old, and shrunken. He sits and rambles on all the time. He rambles on about leaving a dog and about building a tower, and he rambles on some more, but only the stuff about the dog and the tower is true.

He did help build the tower and the dog is still alive. The animal is covered with tangled knots and lies on the mat in front of our door all day whining. It irks Bonnie. She says she gets grubby just *thinking* about the dog, but sometimes she bends down anyway and strokes him, or sets down tender meat for him.

My brother says I exaggerate. "He isn't all that grubby. I've known some other dogs, believe me."

He doesn't want to muddy the thought of home completely. That's why he thinks of me, thinks of Bonnie, who comes to keep me and Edie company when my mother is out, imagines that we are fine under the kitchen lamp with a conversation about nothing, like the one tonight, imagines Edie upstairs in her bed and Boatman's dog outside the door and Boatman in his chair on the path where the good man likes to sit the most. From a distance, you would pay good money for our house. Ivy on the front, pigeons on the roof. My brother wants to go on with them, these pleasant thoughts.

He forgets that Momma is out more than she is home, that Boatman is too much a child to take care of himself and I'm too young to be *allowed* to take care of myself, that Edie is too young for everything but wants to try anything at all, and that Bonnie is doing her best for us. Very happy here we haven't yet managed to become.

Axel doesn't want to think of Boatman's dog. His whining might make him sad because whining is crying, and if he doesn't watch out the thought of last week will pop up again, of when he left, livid blue in the face, and was never coming back.

"What do you mean—did something happen by any chance?" says my brother with a smirk.

I don't think it's funny. I think it is too bad that my brother acts as if he had forgotten chunks of his life. As if he were crossing out what was first written. You can't just cross things out.

It's like the smell of Boatman's dog—you can't get rid of his stench either. The whole kitchen stinks of that dog, even if the door has been open for just a few seconds and the wind isn't even coming from the wrong direction. Bonnie stood a sheet of fiberboard up against the wall of the house and calls the place "his doghouse." There is a plate of dog food under it and a pan of water, but the dog never goes for it. He doesn't want to lie under the fiberboard.

I hope he will eventually get over his whining someday. Bonnie says you get used to it, but you don't.

On account of the dog, there is always sadness lying on the doorstep. And you don't get used to that, because that chunk of sadness gradually becomes a heap of misery we have to step over every time we go out the kitchen door. Or if we want to bring Boatman in.

Bonnie puts her knitting down and sets her cup of tea on top of it. She stirs her tea.

"What's old?" she says, and she smiles. "When are you too old for kids?"

"Oh," I say. "When you turn forty."

"Oh, good," says Bonnie.

"Sure, roughly," I say.

Bonnie keeps smiling. Her spoon glides through her tea. She kisses the cup before she sips from it.

"Then I've still got time," she says, and she licks her lips. "Good."

I hear her, but I'm not listening. I look at my empty hands. I look at the empty chair beside me, where my brother is not sitting.

"It's so quiet in the house," I say. "It's making my skin pull."

"Then make noise," says Bonnie. "Put on some music."

"No," I say.

"Then go do something. Put your thoughts on another track, go write a letter. If I hadn't started a sock, I would think it's exactly the right quiet for a letter." Bonnie nods at me.

"A letter," I say. "It's so late. The idea that my hand will have to move already makes me groan."

"Sis," says Bonnie, as if that were my name.

"That's right, Sis," my brother says in my ear. "You can sit around thinking all the time, or you could just write down what happened *after* last week, because I don't know a thing about that."

"Hokay," I say. "A letter."

Beside the small stack of newspapers on the corner of the table is some paper. I pull it toward me with one finger and lay it in front of myself. I look over my shoulder to see if my brother has seen how white the paper still is.

"How should I start?" I say. "Bonnie is knitting a sock?"

Bonnie nods, with one eye on her work. One of her eyebrows is way up and her mouth is crooked. With a simple movement of her thumb, she shows what she thinks. "Nice beginning," she says.

"Girls, girls," my brother says in my ear. "Just start with Boatman. How are things with the good Boatman? Isn't he cold?"

I look out the window in the door. "Isn't it getting too cold for him, Bonnie?" I say.

Bonnie jerks her eyes up, slightly startled. She sets her cup of tea down on the table. "Cold?" she says. "Are you cold?"

"Not me," I say. "You?"

"Not me," says my brother. "I'm warm, lying with my back against Mortimer."

"Boatman doesn't have a blanket on, that's really what I mean," I say.

Bonnie shrugs her shoulders, smiling, as if she thought it sweet of me to be concerned. "That'll be the day, when that man catches cold," she says. "He's made of leather. And it's plenty warm outside." She grins and leans over, gropes around in the bag beside her feet. She bats balls of yarn every which way and finds what she is looking for: a ball of white. She grins as if she were seeing an old friend again. She lays the yarn against her lips.

"Hmm," she goes.

I lean sideways, against my brother—I think I feel his warmth through my clothes—and look out the window in the door.

Boatman is sitting in his chair on the path. His head bobs back and forth. His mouth doesn't stay still for a second.

"He doesn't stop," I say. "It just goes on. Mumble-mumble, and nobody listens to him. 'I am leaving a dog. I built a tower.'"

"Poor man," says Bonnie. "Where is that tower anyway?"

"Somewhere by the sea. It's a lighthouse."

"A lighthouse," says Bonnie. Her knitting lowers into her lap. She looks at me and nods. "Of course."

The clock over the counter strikes the hour. The little lady comes out, turns on her heel, and disappears again.

I have to think of my mother when that little doll appears: she comes into the kitchen only to show off her clothes, too. Hi, everybody. See you later, everybody. And off she goes again with her pilot.

I look sideways, at my brother, to see if he is thinking about my mother as well. About the fact that, just for now—or is it for always?—he doesn't fit in with her clothes anymore.

My brother's thoughts are set at zero. He is nodding off against my shoulder. He smacks his lips, fights sleep, curls himself up against Mortimer. I wish it were morning, that he were coming down for breakfast, would scratch his head and say, "Good morning," with that little crusty patch on his voice.

"What did you say?" says Bonnie.

"Did I say something?" I say.

"I thought you did," says Bonnie.

I slowly get up. My arms and legs feel limp because I kept them still so as not to wake my brother. I open the kitchen door wide and take a deep breath. Outside, the air is just as thick and hot as inside. The sky is wide and big, the moon is round.

"If you wait for them, one never falls," Bonnie says behind me.

"I wasn't looking at the stars," I say, although I do know of a wish that I wouldn't say out loud and wouldn't write down, just in case.

"You're sweet. But if I had to choose, I'd stay with Mortimer, Sis," Axel says in my ear.

I don't like hearing him say that. Wishes have to come true.

I turn to look at him, expect to see his face, but he has drilled his nose into Mortimer's hair. His mouth is lying right near Mortimer's ear. He is whispering all kinds of sweet things and acts as if his lips were fingers.

"Oh," I say. "You."

I nod at Boatman's dog at my feet and tap his rump with my toe. The creature is lolling in front of the doorstep like a sack of sand that was tossed there, and the only parts of his head that move are his eyebrows and his eyes. He raises his eyebrows, looks at me, and whines softly in the back of his throat. On other days, I would have grumbled that he finally has to give it a rest, but tonight I am also sorrowing a little in the back of my throat.

I bend my knees, squat down, and stroke his head. "You're sweet," I whisper.

This makes the dog calmer. I can tell. I grow calmer too from my stroking hand, from the clicking of Bonnie's knitting needles behind me, and from Boatman rambling on in his chair farther down. "I'm leaving a dog. I built a tower." Mumble-mumble.

There is a tap on my shoulder. I'm thinking, It's my brother, and I'm already smiling as I turn around. But how could I have thought that?

It is Edie.

She is asking for a smile, a coincidence, and she comes and leans up against me with her warm little body.

"Where did you come from?" I say, as if I didn't know. She smells of her bed.

"I can't sleep," she says.

"Look who's here," Bonnie sings from the kitchen.

"Edie," I sing.

My eyes follow the downspout that runs up through the ivy to the roof, past Edie's window. Those ten feet down she has once again managed in absolute quiet.

"She did it again," I say to Bonnie behind me.

"Yes, I see," Bonnie calls back. "She knows that she's supposed to be careful. If she falls, we're not going to glue the pieces back together."

"You're telling," says Edie quietly, and she squeezes between my legs. "You're not allowed to tell."

My lap is unstable. I squat, leaning lightly against the doorjamb, but I don't tell her. She will just have to notice on her own that her chair is moving.

"I'm not telling. I'm watching out for you," I say as I throw my arm around her. "You and your climbing all the time. I have to take care that you don't do anything dangerous."

"Sure, sure, you have nothing better to do."

I catch her by the back of her head and turn her face toward me. I knit my eyebrows and look at her mouth, to see if it hasn't changed.

"You're getting close to being rude," I say, and I have

to smile a little because of her.

"No," says Edie.

"Yessiree," I say.

"Stop it," says Axel. "That's how the biggest arguments start. With yes and no. Yes and no, yes and no, and smack." He points at his eye, which is still discolored. He takes my hand and touches his eyebrows with my fingertips.

"What were you doing?" says Edie.

I rub my eye. I say, "Not much."

"I'm not doing much either," says Edie.

"Hm," I sing. "I was thinking about our Axel."

"Me too, all the time," says Edie.

I hear Axel groan. We make him uneasy. If he were standing here with his suitcases, ready to leave, and Edie and I were to repeat what we just said, pulling the faces we just did, he would set his bags on the ground and stay home.

"I know," I say.

He swallows a few times and snuggles closer against Mortimer in search of comfort. Any closer is impossible.

Edie accidentally brought an earwig along. There are also cobwebs and leaf remnants in the crocheted smock of her nightie. I pluck at them. My hands grow soft from plucking. After a while, they caress more than pluck.

I have to hug Edie.

"I think of him almost all day," she says with her face very close to mine, and with an emphasis on "all day," as if I had asked her how often she thinks of him. "Until I fall asleep I think of him, if I can sleep at all."

I close my eyes for a few seconds, and I imagine that Edie's head is my brother's head. I change into Mortimer, and Axel hums very quietly against me, the way he always hums when he's feeling neither sad nor happy.

"Watch out," says Edie. She pinches my upper arm because she almost fell off my lap.

"Watch out," says Axel.

"Got you!" I say, and I save her. It takes a while before I come down from high up in the clouds and land on the kitchen doorstep.

"I almost fell flat," says Edie to the kitchen.

"So you almost had to be glued after all?" says Bonnie.

Edie giggles. In her mind, she's a little porcelain angel. I am sure of it, because that's how she's looking at herself, and she is imagining what it would be like to be lying there smashed to bits. She giggles from deep down in her stomach. She makes me laugh.

Axel hears me and grins. After a little while, it's a grinning laugh. He's lying against Mortimer shaking. Soon Mortimer will wake up, and Mortimer will also start shaking. We'll go around the whole world that way. Axel has a contagious laugh. All kinds of things scrape in his throat then, and you get the feeling that you're being tickled. I don't know how it happens, but you just start growing with pleasure.

I jump. I believe I said his name.

Bonnie and Edie heard nothing. Edie's mouth hangs open, and her ears are big enough. She is staring at Boatman. She smacks a few times to wet her tongue and suddenly asks more loudly than necessary—so, asking Bonnie—when we're going to go and see his tower.

Bonnie doesn't respond. Her thoughts are somewhere else.

"We'll do that someday," I say for her. "Take the stairs up, and then you'll be able to look out over the sea, because it's by the sea. It's a fire beacon."

Edie doesn't realize it, but she lets her surprise speak as soon as she hears the word "fire."

"Huh?" she goes.

"No," I say so she has to look at me. "They used to use fire. Bundles of sticks at a time. Now they use a lamp. The light is so high up that you can see it from far away."

Edie sits quietly looking up at me as I make a spinning motion above my head with my arm and act as if my face were the light.

"But why?" says Edie.

"Yes, why," I say.

I don't know. Lighthouses stand there. They have always stood there.

I hesitate, start my sentence before I know how I'm going to finish it. "Either because ships want to know where the land that they have to get to is, or because ships want to know where the land they have to stay away from is. That's why."

Edie looks as if she didn't understand even the shortest words. She runs her tongue over her lips and lets herself hang heavily on my arm.

"Yeah," she says slowly. "But when do they know which one they want?"

"That depends on the ships," I say. "The one they want is the one they will see."

"Yeah."

She thinks this is hard. I can hear her brain working. In her mind, whole fleets are going down. Other boats enter a harbor that is decorated with little flags. Edie imitates in miniature my movements of just before. Her thumb is the light and the forefinger of her other hand turns around the light. She plays watch out, go away-hi there, come here. "And does it always turn out all right?"

I kiss her on her temple. "Yes, it usually turns out all right," I say. "There are only a few ships that misunderstand."

"There are hardly *any* ships that misunderstand.

Don't say strange things to that child. Next, she'll be dreaming about it," says Bonnie. She pushes her chair back and yawns. She needs all her muscles for it. "Just sometimes a boat goes missing, Edie, and very sometimes one will run into a cliff, but they're the dumb ones. And *you* have to put your slippers on."

"Sure," says Edie.

I push my little sister away, so she is forced to stand up. Bonnie and I both look at her so she can't try to think up something else. There are no more earwigs that need to move to new homes. All the cobwebs are gone from her nightie.

"Slippers," says Bonnie.

Edie runs on her pattering bare feet through the kitchen. She sticks out her stomach. It has to take the place of her tongue, as she would prefer to stick out her tongue. She doesn't dare because of Bonnie's impatient hands.

"Slippers, slippers," she says.

Bonnie and I look at each other. We are two mothers. We hear the soft gluey sound of Edie's feet and we melt.

"Aw," says Bonnie. She takes a step forward.

"Don't look," says Axel.

Bonnie does. Her gaze skates across the tile floor, lingers at her feet. She represses a yawn.

"Don't," says Axel.

She does. With the toe of her sandal she traces a joint. She looks up. It takes a moment before she says anything.

"It's still there," she says.

I nod.

"Blood makes tough stains," I say.

Axel rolls away from Mortimer. He lies on his back, pushes the sheet completely off himself. He wipes the sweat from his chest.

"So now you guys are talking about it again anyway," he says. He quietly shakes his head and draws the corners of his mouth in. How is it possible, is what he means. It wasn't all that bad. He doesn't regret anything. He managed to get Momma's pilot of a week—"Don't exaggerate, I've known him longer than that"—against the tiles.

"It was his own fault," says Bonnie. "Comes into the house more than ten feet for the first time ever and calls Axel every filthy name under the sun, until the boy is about to hit the ceiling."

I kneel down. Beside the door is a chair and that's what I lean on, as if it were Axel's side of the bed in Charlestown. The sweater hanging over the back of the chair is Axel's arm.

"I can take it. I can take a punch or two. I wouldn't even mind getting two black eyes over it."

"Did he say that?" says Bonnie.

"Yes," I say. "And he wants us to be sure to do what Momma said. If she doesn't want anyone to breathe a single word about him anymore, then Axel thinks that we should be good and do as we're told. Not a word. Not you, not Edie, not me."

"We'll be declared saints yet," Bonnie sighs. "That woman."

Exactly. That woman. She just does as she likes. Another year and I won't breathe a word about my mother.

Bonnie wants to toss her sock with the knitting needles on it into her knitting basket, but she forgets to. She suddenly isn't moving anymore, just cocks her ears and says, "Shh. Was that the attic stairs?"

"I don't know," I say.

I didn't hear anything.

Bonnie's head moves every which way, my way too.

I grow hot and cold. Maybe I made another sound by accident? Did I say something strange? For a few seconds, the blood drains from my face because Bonnie points with a nod at somewhere behind the open door and says almost without a voice, "Oh. Look."

The air from outside falls on the back of my neck. I hear Bonnie say he's calling me. I swallow. What does she mean?

"He's calling you."

I follow the movements of her mouth. It doesn't surprise me that Axel is calling me. It doesn't surprise me that Bonnie hears Axel too. Bonnie hears him just as I do in her head. Of course, we're connected.

I place my hand on my cheek because I have to know

where my head is. My eyes and ears are bigger than I am. I don't hear anything out of the ordinary, but when Bonnie says that somebody is calling me, then that will be the way it is. I see that she is looking past me with a smile, is walking in the direction that the sound is coming from.

"You see that? He's calling you," she says.

I have to look around.

I must be disappointed.

Of course Axel's not there.

At the end of the path sits Boatman. He is calling me with his hand. He is reaching his arm out in my direction. As usual, he is shaking his head, so that as usual he seems dissatisfied or to be saying No without words.

I crumble, curse once, but forget to curse some more, because suddenly I hear Boatman's voice.

He is not rambling. He is not saying that he is leaving a dog. He is not saying that he built a lighthouse. He is not mumbling. He is saying obviously and clearly for him, "Where is your brother?"

Where. Is. Your. Brother.

"Gone, Boatman," I say.

"Where to?"

"To, uh... Charlestown," I say. "But we're not allowed to..."

"To Charlestown?" he says. "What's he doing over there in Charlestown?"

I shrug my shoulders and look at Bonnie, who is smiling, keeping her lips tightly sealed.

"What's he doing over there? Dancing?"

"Maybe," I say.

"Why's he doing that in Charlestown?" says Boatman. He slumps in his chair, as if he had to recover and needed time to think. A moment later he says that my brother can dance here as well. In Charlestown, they may know how to dance, but dancing my brother can also do here. Who let him go to Charlestown? A boy like that can dance here too, can't he? Why did he have to go to Charlestown?

I bite my lip. Otherwise I'll start grinning. Next, Boatman will forget about his dog and his tower. Next, he'll think, just as I do, of nothing but Charlestown.

Next, he'll be repeating that word the whole time, tonight and early tomorrow morning and the day after and still when my mother and her pilot happen to be home. He'll just keep repeating it all the time, until we get itchy because it gets on our nerves, particularly my mother and her pilot.

Bonnie steps over Boatman's dog and walks over to his chair.

"You are right, sir," she says. "I don't understand what Axel is doing in Charlestown, either. I can't say it often enough."

She looks over her shoulder in my direction, and she winks, and Boatman literally repeats the last thing Bonnie said. What is Axel doing in Charlestown? What's a boy like that doing there? What can you do there that you can't do here?

"I can't understand, either, why our Axel would go look elsewhere with his Mortimer for what he can find here as well."

Boatman shakes his head as if he disagreed with her, but the opposite is true. He tries to look around, he tries to look up, he tries to grin at Bonnie and say all kinds of things at once. "Sure, if you can also find it here."

"Easy, easy," says Bonnie.

I want to bend over to lift Boatman's dog a little way off the ground and move him aside, because Bonnie wants to pass with the wheelchair, but my hands hover in midair. I turn my head—does Bonnie see what's happening?

"You are right, Boatman," she says, and she briefly touches his shoulder so he knows she's talking to him. "You are more than absolutely right."

Only then does her face change. Only then does she see what is happening. She slowly lifts up her arm and moans in surprise. She points to show Boatman where to look.

Boatman's jaw drops in mid sentence.

His dog, who during an entire day gets moving maybe only during the last few seconds, pushes himself up on his paws with a moan and tries to recall how he was supposed to stretch his body. He arches his back, shakes his head. He squeaks all the while. His joints hurt.

Suddenly he notices that we are looking at him. He looks back: at Boatman, at Bonnie, at me. He doesn't wag his tail. He seems to be nodding at us and letting us see how it's supposed to be done, easy, easy. He hobbles down the path. There are slippers on his paws, and one of his ears is heavier than the other. He walks bent with age, and he walks crookedly because his front end is slower than his back end.

Bonnie and I exchange glances.

The dog knows where he is going. Everything about him is determined. There is such a thing, slowly determined. He has thought it over for hours.

He walks out on our little lawn, the widest open space we have. It is the size of a rug, trimmed with flowers, but the dog turns it into a carpet that was rolled out especially for him.

He sits down with his back to us, as if he didn't want to see us. He counts to ten and only then looks around and makes it clear that he is not sitting with his back to us. He is sitting facing the moon. That's it.

"Jesus," says Bonnie.

"Yes," I say. I hear it too. My ears are as good as hers. The hairs on my arms stand on end.

At first from very far away, but then from deep in the throat of Boatman's dog, comes a mournful howl. I have never before heard crying so quiet. Tears fill my eyes. "Jesus."

I look around at the empty kitchen, at the table where my brother is not sitting. Axel has sat straight up in bed. He has pulled up his knees. He is holding his head in his hands.

Bonnie doesn't see Axel. She sees only the dog. She has thrown her arms around herself and tries to rub herself warm with her hands. She wants to act as if she were smiling, but she doesn't manage.

She walks carefully, as if barefoot, down the gravel path. Halfway, she looks around—am I following her?

I nod at her.

Boatman's dog drops his head again as if he were looking for air on the ground. Slowly he raises his snout. He purses his lips almost like a human. He carefully lets go of the sound. He falteringly sends his howl to the moon, but it doesn't carry very far. It spreads like a breeze. It is thin. A jacket flapping over the yard and the house for a moment.

Bonnie and I take hold of each other's arms. Our skin is goose bumps. Our throats are blocked. We have to try to smile, even though we only half manage. We rub each other's backs and squeeze each other's hands.

I hope that Mortimer is awake. I hope that he blinks his eyes drunk with sleep and sees Axel's back beside him. I hope that his hand caresses Axel's back, and that his voice caresses as well. That he caressingly asks what's wrong.

"Nothing."

No, Axel's not lying.

"Homesickness," he says.

Mortimer sits up.

"Shh."

Bonnie wraps her arm around my head and pushes my face against her blouse.

I get almost no air. I shrug my shoulders so Bonnie knows that I'm almost suffocating but that I don't mind.

She strokes my back in her way, as if she were playing guitar on it. She could keep that up for a long time. She could also sing doing it, the way she sings. "It'll be all right. It'll be all right. It will."

Her voice goes still, her hand too. In her chest, where my head lies against it, I hear her breath catch. I hear her say, "Jesus," very quietly. "Jesus. You should see the two of them now."

She lets me go so I can see what she means.

My face is crumpled and my eyelids stick together, but I rub them until I am back in the yard and can look around.

The first thing my eye catches is Boatman. He is waiting in his wheelchair in front of the kitchen door. The light from inside stands out around him like a little room. I hear him mumbling. He says he has built a tower. He says he is leaving a dog. He says that they know how to dance in Charlestown. But what else is a boy like that supposed to do there? What can you do there that you can't do here?

I have to smile. I have to smile a really broad smile. I

show all my teeth, because about twelve feet above Boatman's head, while he is sitting there shut up inside himself, always mumbling the same thing, sits Edie. He doesn't see her, and she doesn't look at him.

She is not looking at anybody. She is a little white angel that is also shut up inside herself. She is sitting up on the roof gutter, seriously staring ahead. With her arm, she makes a spinning motion above her head. She turns and turns. She thinks her face is radiating light. Now it is. Now it's not.

"Edie!" I exclaim. "Edie, what are you doing? That's not allowed!"

"Why not?" she calls back. She doesn't stop turning and radiating light. The ships have to understand her right.

"Because it's dangerous. Come down. Come here!"

"Sure!" she calls back. "Come here! Come here!"

"Jesus," Bonnie says to me. She giggles and yammers something I don't understand because her lips are taut with smiling. She takes a few steps toward the house. She has to be our mother, thinks so herself. One time she has to feed an old dog, another time she has to help Boatman, and then another time she has to comfort me or get Edie down from the roof gutter.

A few feet farther she stands still.

Boatman's dog crosses her path.

She looks down at him, watches him return to the house.

He shuffles, takes all the time in the world, hangs his head, and looks up from under his eyebrows. His gaze says that he actually doesn't know what he just did anymore.

Bonnie and I follow him to the kitchen door, where he turns around three times and finally becomes a doormat again.

Bonnie turns toward me. She lifts up her arms and reaches her hands out to me in question. The way she is standing there she seems to be indicating us all.

"Can it do any harm?" she says.

No, I think. Very happy we haven't yet managed to become here, but it could be worse. Bonnie is knitting a sock. Edie is sitting on the roof. Boatman is talking to nobody in particular. His dog is howling at the moon.

That will be a nice letter.

I look over my shoulder at Axel—does he see us?

No.

He is already sleeping, deeply, with his back against Mortimer's stomach.